Poppy Field

Poppy Field

Michael Morpurgo
Illustrated by Michael Foreman

SCHOLASTIC

Scholastic Children's Books
An imprint of Scholastic Ltd
Euston House, 24 Eversholt Street, London, NW1 1DB, UK
Registered office: Westfield Road, Southam, Warwickshire, CV47 0RA
SCHOLASTIC and associated logos are trademarks
and/or registered trademarks of Scholastic Inc.
First published in the UK by Scholastic Ltd, 2018

Afterword photo credits:
P.52 John McCrae and Poem – FF9P7E: Granger Historical Picture Archive/Alamy Stock Photo
P.52–53 Poppies bloom in Flanders Fields by brick wall – Jack Taylor/Getty Images
P.55 Moina Michaels – F1WD8H: Lee Karen Stow/Alamy Stock Photo
P.56 Poppies bloom in Flanders Fields – Jack Taylor/Getty Images
P.58 Poppy – Imperial War Museums (EPH 2313) – Imperial War Museum
P.59 Earl Haigs Poppy Appeal – Keystone France-Gamma Keystone – Getty images
P.60 Making poppies at Poppy Factory 1922 – Poppy Factory
P.60 (inset) Poppy Factory employees with HRH The Prince of Wales – Poppy factory
P.62–63 Tyne Cot – Ian Dickens
P.64 Remembrance ceremony – Andrew Cowie/AFP/Getty Images
P.67 Soldier's helmet on gun – Christopher Furlong/Getty Images
P.68–69 Behind the scenes of British Legion Poppy Factory – Scott Barbour/Getty Images

The right of Michael Morpurgo and Michael Foreman to be identified
as the author and illustrator of this work has been asserted by them.

HB ISBN: 978 1 407 18142 4
PB ISBN: 978 1 407 18941 3

A CIP catalogue record for this book
is available from the British Library.

Printed in Malaysia
Papers used by Scholastic Children's Books are made
from wood grown in sustainable forests.

1 3 5 7 9 10 8 6 4 2

www.scholastic.co.uk

For Voices at the Door

— MM

We are the Dead. Short days ago

We lived, felt dawn, saw sunset glow,

Loved and were loved, and now we lie

In Flanders fields

My name is Martens Merkel. I live on a farm in Flanders, with my mother and my grandfather. I go to school in Poperinge, just a few kilometres away. I cycle there if the weather isn't too bad. All around us are the battlefields of the First World War, which ended a long time ago, in 1918. You wouldn't know it was a battlefield now, that the trenches ran right through our farm, that where the cows now graze was No Man's Land.

Poppies grow here in their millions, so thick sometimes in the wheat field in the valley that you can barely see the wheat for the poppies. We all call it just "Poppy Field". So, one way or another, poppies have been part of my life, of all our lives, ever since I can remember – and before that even, as you will see.

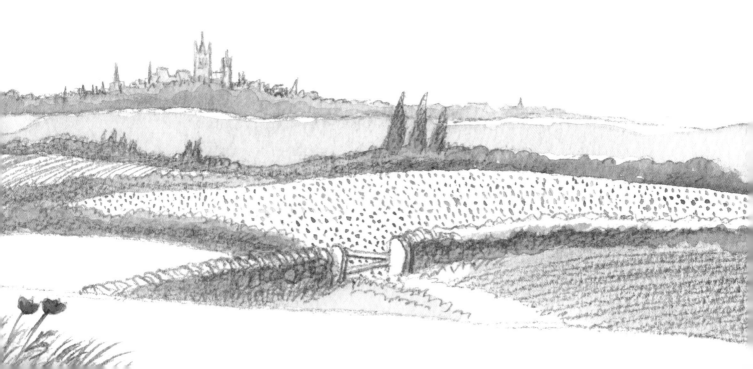

It's very quiet here, just birdsong in the morning early and the milking parlour humming twice a day, a place of small woods and neat fields, and lanes like ribbons running through the farmland. Very few cars, very few people. Wide skies over a landscape of gentle hills and valleys, the towers and spires of Ypres in the distance.

You would only know there had ever been a war here from the cemeteries and memorials. There are dozens of them, hundreds

probably. I've never counted them. We can see two of them from the house, go past them almost every day, one for British soldiers, one for Germans. Most of my friends hardly notice the cemeteries, because they're always there, part of the landscape. I notice them, but then I have good reason to. Because that same war killed my father, and that was 11 years ago, in the spring of 2005. That's 87 years after the war ended.

Papa died just after I was born, so I only know him from photographs. Everyone tells me he was a very kind man, a good farmer, who loved his cows, and his tractor, and his land. He was as kind to his land as he was to everyone, Grandpa once told me. Grandpa says other farmers would have got rid of the poppies, sprayed them with weedkiller, because they certainly spoil the wheat crop. But to Papa poppies weren't weeds. Papa was killed ploughing the land he loved, ploughing Poppy Field. His tractor drove over an unexploded shell. A British or a German one, no one knows, and it doesn't matter. Mama doesn't speak of him hardly at all, because it upsets her too much. But Grandpa likes to talk about him and I like it when he does. He brings Papa alive for me.

Papa lies in the village cemetery now. I go with Mama and Grandpa to lay flowers on his grave on his birthday, May 22nd, and on All Souls and Christmas Day too. We cycle there, past the war cemeteries. They remind me that every one of those soldiers lying there under those stones and crosses had a mother and a father, like Grandpa, a sister or a brother, a wife, like Mama, or a son like me.

Papa was born here, as I was, grew up on the farm, which was a battlefield, died on it. He died as they all did, in a way, because of accident of birth. Those soldiers who lie in all the war cemeteries round about here were born in Britain, or Germany, or Austria, France, Belgium, Canada, India, New Zealand, Jamaica, Australia, America. They came from all over the world. They came here, to fight on one side or the other, depending simply on where they were born. They fought in a huge and terrible war, the war to end all wars they called it, which happened so long ago now that no one is old enough to remember it.

I'm not old enough to remember Papa. I know him only through those photographs and through the story Grandpa tells me. Grandpa has told me this story over and over again. It is really several stories in one, one long family story, full of strange meetings. He has told me

more than once that he likes to tell me the story, because it was the story he used to tell Papa when he was my age.

I am very like Papa in so many ways – Grandpa often says that – and not just to look at. It's also because Papa was a bit of a dreamer, like me. It was because Papa knew and loved this story so much, Grandpa reckons, that Papa always looked after Poppy Field so well.

Papa loved that field more than anywhere else in the world, and not just because of the poppies, but because of all that had happened in that valley a long time ago.

I like to stand there outside the milking parlour, look down across the valley at Poppy Field and imagine it all, especially when the poppies are out and blowing in the wind.

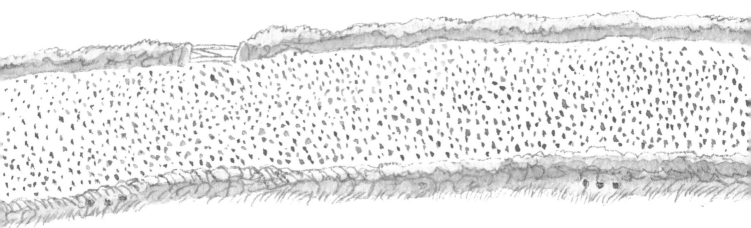

Sometimes it feels as if the whole field is alive, swaying, dancing. But even so, I keep my distance. To hear and know the story is one thing, but I could never bring myself to go and stand in the place where it had happened. Mama has not set foot in Poppy Field either, not since the day Papa died. Grandpa has to go there. He does all the machine work on the farm now, all the ploughing and tilling and harvesting that Papa used to do. Mama looks after the calves and the poultry, and the cheesemaking mostly. And I help Grandpa with the milking at weekends, after school. We walk the farm together, check the animals. I love those walks.

It's usually on one of these walks that he likes to tell me the story. I know it so well by now, know exactly what's going to happen, but I love to hear it. It's our story, my story, the family story. The trunk of the fallen tree by the duck pond – which had once been a shell hole from the First World War – that's Grandpa's favourite storytelling place. You look out across the whole farm from there.

"That scrap of writing paper in the frame hanging in the hallway may not look like much, Martens, but it's the beginning of the whole story."

This is how Grandpa starts the story – with the "scrap of paper", as he calls it. I hardly ever pass it by without noticing it, and I often stop to read it. It's a poem, and not at all easy to read, because it's written in smudged and faded pencil, and in English too, on scrunched-up paper that has been flattened out, and the paper is heavily stained. I know the poem by heart, we all do, Grandpa, Mama and me. It was the most important poem in Papa's life too, they said. He knew it off by heart as well.

Before I ever learnt any English at school I could recite it.

In Flanders fields the poppies grow,

Between the crosses row on row

And in the sky, the ~~wrens~~ larks

Still bravely singing,

Fly scarce ~~heard~~ amidst the guns below.
heard

Short days ago,

We lived, felt dawn, saw ~~the~~ sunset glow,

Loved and were loved,

And now we lie in Flanders Fields

The writing is full of corrections and crossings out. I did not know or understand when I first learnt this poem how famous it was, but because of Grandpa's story I did know how it came to be hanging here in the hallway of our house.

Sometimes I reach out and touch the poem, for luck, as I leave the house, if I have a test at school, or an exam. I see Grandpa doing the same sometimes, Mama too. It's a sort of family ritual. The poem is up there in the hall by the front door, with the photo of Papa nearby, on the table. There is always a poppy beside that photo, a fresh one, wild from the field, or when they aren't growing, one that Mama had knitted herself.

This is how Grandpa tells the story, not word for word, of course, but how I remember him telling it.

My mama, that's your great-grandmother, Martens – Marie, she was called – she was the one who found the poem. Marie was just a girl, about eight years old when the war came, the First World War that is, a long time before she met my father, your great-grandfather. Her family lived on a farm on the other side of Ypres, near a village called Brielen, not far from a field hospital – known as Essex Farm to the soldiers. "Tommies" the soldiers were always called. Many of the farming folk around Ypres and the townsfolk too, come to that, had already left. Ypres and everywhere around was in range of German guns and was often being bombarded. Half the town was in ruins already.

But Marie's family decided it was safer to stay. Her father, wounded in the war, invalided out of the Belgian army, had seen the misery of the thousands of refugees on the roads, with nowhere to go. At least if they stayed at home they could feed themselves, he thought. Better to stay together, shelter in the cellar, sell a few eggs and chickens, some hay and straw to the Tommies. He thought they could just about manage to get by, and they did.

He would send Marie up to the Field Hospital each day with a basket of eggs to sell. She was good at it too. It was a matter of pride to her to come home each time with her money jingling in her pocket, and her basket empty. The Tommies at the Field Hospital got used to seeing her, liked to see her. "The little poppy girl", they came to call her. And here's why.

It was springtime, the spring of 1915, and the poppies were blooming along the farm tracks, along the edges of the fields, so Marie would always pick a few on the way. She would have quite a bunch by the time she got there.

She loved poppies, but that wasn't the only reason she picked
them. The truth was that she discovered the Tommies liked them, that
if she offered them a poppy or two as well, they would be more likely
to buy her eggs. But this morning there were not many soldiers about
up at the Field Hospital, and those that were there were busy carrying
stretchers, seeing to the wounded. No one had time that day for the
little poppy girl with her basket of eggs.

Then she spotted a soldier on his own, sitting on a chair near the back of an ambulance, pencil in hand, a notebook on his knee. He was intent on his writing. She had seen him before, and had often noticed that he was a lot older than most of the other soldiers. She walked right up to him.

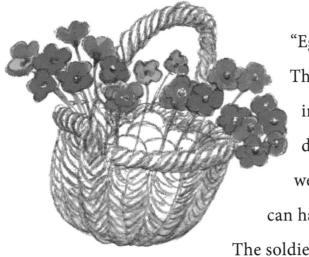

"Eggs, Tommy?" she said, in English. Those were about the only two words in English she knew. The soldier didn't seem to hear her at first. So she went on, in Flemish this time. "You can have a poppy if you like as well."

The soldier looked up then, irritated at this intrusion. He tore out a page from the notepad, scrunched it up and threw it away. It landed in a nearby puddle and floated.

Marie bent down to pick it up. Paper was useful for lighting the fire – that was her first thought. A child living like her in the rubble and ruin of war had long ago learnt to throw nothing away, that everything has its uses.

The soldier seemed to know that, to read her mind. "Keep it," he told her. "It's only good for lighting fires." He spoke some Flemish, and Marie was surprised at that. The Tommies always expected you to speak English. She saw now that there was writing on the paper. "It's a poem," the soldier said. "I can't get it right. But I have to. It's for my best friend. For all of them, I suppose. Over there." He pointed to a newly dug grave nearby. "He was killed yesterday. We just buried him."

"Lieutenant Alexis Helmer. Alex. Tell you what, little poppy girl, if you would lay a few of your poppies on his grave for me, that would be kind. I'd do it myself, but I hurt my ankle yesterday, tripped over. Not much of a soldier, eh? Tripping over. Clumsy old fellow. I can't walk all that well this morning. I don't really want eggs, just the poppies. Alex loved poppies."

So that's what your great-grandmother Marie did, Martens. She walked over to the newly dug grave, crouched down and laid some of her poppies on it. When she turned round, the soldier was holding out a coin, offering it to her. She wouldn't take it. "Poppies grow wild,"

she told him. "They belong to everyone. You sure you don't want eggs?"

He smiled. "Very well, two eggs, then." He paid her, and took them. He seemed not to want to talk any more, and after gazing for a while at the poppies on the grave, that were now being blown away one by one by the breeze, he began writing again.

She left him, sold a few more eggs to the cook at the Field Hospital – always her best customer – and was back home on the farm before she realized she still had the scrap of paper in her pocket. She told everyone at home about the soldier and the poem, how she had laid the poppies on the grave of his best friend, and how sad it was. Her mama, being a schoolteacher, knew a little English. She read the poem out, translating it for them as she went along. When she had finished no one spoke for some time, until Marie did.

"It is beautiful," she said. And that was when she saw the tears on her father's face. She had never in all her life seen him cry before.

"You say he threw this away?" her mama said.

"He said I could keep it," Marie told her.

"Then you shall, Marie," she said, smoothing the scrap of paper out on the table. "I think these are precious words, and we should treasure them, look after them."

So that's what they did. They found a broken old frame in the
corner of the cellar where they were all living. Marie's father mended it

as best he could, and then hung the poem up on the wall. It became
like a talisman for them. They would touch it every morning, like we
do to this day, like I've seen you do, Martens. They came to believe
that if anything could see them through those terrible times, the
horrors, the hunger, the cold, the shelling, it would be this poem. In
time Marie's mama taught them all to speak it and learn it, Marie herself,

Marie's papa, the whole family. The soldier's poem up on the wall gave them strength and hope, helped them to survive. And survive they did.

And this was just the first strange meeting in the story, Martens, the soldier poet and the little poppy girl. I have always thought it might well have saved her life, saved all their lives. I do know for a fact that without the next strange meeting I would not be here telling you this story; and come to that, Max, you wouldn't be here listening to it either.

That poem stayed in Marie's head, as childhood things do, and the scrap of paper still hung in its frame on the wall in their farmhouse, now rebuilt after the war. It was about ten years after the war ended in November of 1918 that it happened, the next strange meeting. Marie, not a little girl any more, quite grown up by now, met a young man in Ypres. Piet, he was called – later to be my father, and your great-grandfather. He was a farmer's son, from the country outside Ypres, but living in the town now, helping to rebuild it, and he was one of the Town Fire Brigade too.

Every evening to honour and remember those who died, the men from the Town Fire Brigade sounded their bugles under the Menin Gate – you know it well enough, Martens, that huge memorial arch in town where the walls are covered with the names of the thousands of soldiers who have no known grave. Marie always said that's where she first fell in love with Piet, watching him and listening to him as he and his friends played their bugles.

Well, this is the story of how they met. When Marie had finished her day's work at market selling their farm produce – eggs and butter and cheese – she would sometimes pass by the Menin Gate to hear the bugles play. She would stand there and remember the faces of the Tommy soldiers at the Field Hospital, the graves newly dug, row upon row of them, and the soldier poet who had thrown away his scrap of paper.

One evening, as she stood there watching the buglers playing, as she was remembering, her eyes came to rest on one of them. He reminded her at once of her soldier poet. The bugles rang out loud under the great archway, and she felt tears behind her eyes as she often did. As the echoes died away, there came a voice, speaking these words.

"*In Flanders fields the poppies blow...*"

She thought at first the voice came from inside her head. She saw who it was then, a soldier in uniform, a Tommy uniform, standing beside the tallest of the buglers, who looked so like the soldier poet she remembered.

The soldier's voice was wavering as he continued.

"*Between the crosses, row on row...*"

Marie found she was speaking the words to herself, mouthing them, and still looking at her bugler, until she found he was now looking back at her. The poem was almost word for word the same, but went on longer beyond the verses Marie knew. She was puzzling over this, over why it was the same but different, as she was walking away back into town. This was when she realized she was not alone. The bugler was walking alongside her.

"You knew that poppy poem, didn't you?" he said. "I saw your lips moving."

"I met the man who wrote it," she told him, "when I was little."

"You do know, don't you, that is just about the most famous poem ever written about war," he told her.

"No," Marie said. "I didn't." She looked up at him. "He was a bit like you. Older maybe. He bought a couple of my eggs, liked my poppies too. I never saw him again."

Sitting in a cafe with him a while later, she found herself telling him the whole story.

"And that scrap of paper," he said, "you've still got it?"

They cycled together back to Marie's farm that same evening, and stood there reading the poem silently in the hallway.

"I'm so glad I met you," he said.

"Me too," she told him, and she reached out and touched the poem. "It's for luck. You should touch it too." And he did.

Six months later, Marie, my mother of course, and Piet, my father – your grandma and your grandpa – were married. Later they moved into this farm, bringing the poem with them, of course, where it hung in the hall of the farmhouse, and a year or so after this I turned up, so that's sixty years ago. Those two worked the farm, rebuilt a lot of the farm buildings, filled in the trenches and shell holes, brought the land back to health, replanted the trees. And I did the same after them, when my turn came, working the land, putting it to rights. Took a lot of doing, still does, come to that. This land needs healing still, Martens, still does. So much needs healing.

Then, as we all know, Martens, another war came raging through twenty years later. They called this one the Second World War – more destruction, more horrors, more grieving. I learnt one thing from that war. They can take over your land, Martens, occupy, march in your streets, fly their flags, but they can't take over your spirit.

Anyway, to cut a long war short, come 1947 with the Second World War over, I found myself a wife, or she found me – let's just say we found each other. Strange meeting that was too, like an echo of another meeting, if you see what I'm saying. She came visiting from England, like a lot of British people do, and was singing in a choir, folk songs. She played the violin, and sang like an angel. I was playing the bugle in the Town Fire Brigade, like my father before me. And one evening I saw her standing there under the Menin Gate watching me.

She came right up to me afterwards and invited me to her concert the next day outside the Cloth Hall. Lovely music it was too. But I hadn't gone there for the music. Kate Moffat, your grandma, Martens, swept me off my feet. I think she liked my uniform.

For many happy years we were together, your grandma and me, and Emile, our little boy, your papa. Of course she loved the poppy poem in the hallway and the story of how it came to be there. Like everyone else by now, she knew that famous poem of John McCrae's well enough. There were postcards of it everywhere in town, on memorials, in books. She came to love Poppy Field specially, her favourite place on the farm. She would speak the poem out loud down there sometimes, as we walked  through the poppy field down to the stream, then up into the woods and back again.

We loved that field. It was our place.

Come ploughing time each year we kept on finding this and that buried in the fields about the farm, the debris of war it was – and we found more of it in Poppy Field than anywhere else, buttons and buckles off the uniforms, bullets, yes, and bones too. It was your grandma, Martens, who found out what had happened there, and once we knew, it made the place even more special to us. She had a friend

who worked in the museum in Ypres, which, it so happens, is named after that poem in the hallway, "In Flanders Fields". The poem was that well known by now. He was the one who verified that our scrap of paper, the poem in the hallway, was indeed written by the hand of John McCrae. So the family story I had grown up with really was true – which we knew anyway – but now it was officially true.

And he was the
one also who told us that Poppy Field
was one of the places in No Man's Land where German
and British soldiers had met together during the Christmas Truce of
1914, exchanged gifts, swapped badges and stories of family and home,
played a game of football, sung carols across No Man's Land way into
Christmas night.

Which was why, once we knew that, we would go out there on every Christmas night, your grandma, your papa and me, and stand there, looking out over the valley, and we would sing a carol to them, to all the soldiers, on both sides.

Then your grandma, my Kate, got sick and died some years before you were born, Martens, as you know. How I wish you had known her. How I wish she had known you. For Emile, for your papa, as a small boy growing up, Poppy Field was a haven for him, a refuge from the sadness of the world, a place of treasured memories.

If ever I could not find him, I would go looking in Poppy Field, and there in amongst the poppies I would find him. When I asked him why he kept going there, he said that was where his mama was, with the poppies. We would still sing a carol out there together on Christmas night, but how I missed your grandma, on those nights specially.

A few years later – and as you get older, Martens, the years pass by so swiftly – Emile had grown out of being a boy and was a man now, working the farm alongside me, and married to your mama. So now there were three of us again, singing carols together under the stars on Christmas night. As you know, your mama can sing like a bird on a mountain, so clear and pure a sound that Emile and I had sometimes to stop singing with her and simply listen in wonder.

And this is where you come into the story, Martens, my grandson, their son. It was a happy, happy day. 'Course, you kept us awake a bit at nights, but that's what babies do. You were so small, Martens, your fingers specially, but they were strong fingers. You gripped like you'd never let go. And all was well – the farm and the family, all of us, in good heart.

And then one morning, the Christmas after you were born, your papa comes in for breakfast, sits down at the kitchen table and tells us this story, how he'd been down to Poppy Field – and that in itself was strange, he said, because he didn't even know why he had gone there.

He was just drawn there. There was a mist rising all along the valley as the sun came up, he said. He had never seen a morning of such beauty. He found himself walking through this mist, when he heard voices. Then he saw them, he told us, just as surely he was seeing us, two men walking towards one another, tentatively, meeting, then standing there talking, smoking, two soldiers from the First World War in greatcoats, one khaki and one grey. He watched them for a while, saw them shaking hands, then walking away from one another. "It happened, honest to God," your papa told us, "right before my eyes."

For days afterwards he was quiet, your papa, and we knew where his thoughts were. Then he puts on his boots after breakfast one morning just a few days later, to go ploughing in Poppy Field, mist still over the valley. I help him hitch up the plough in the farmyard, your mama comes out with his thermos of coffee, and we watch him drive away on the tractor,

watch him disappear into the mist. And that was it. We never saw him
again. Another casualty of the First World War, one more to add to the
millions. You lose a father, Martens, I lose a son, your mama loses a

husband. He used to say, your papa, that he reckoned that in Poppy
Field when it's in full bloom, there must be a poppy growing for every
soldier that died in that war, on all sides, ten million or more.

"In Flanders fields the poppies blow..."

And that's how Grandpa ends the story, with our family poem, as the poet wrote it for great-grandma Marie all those years ago. I say the rest of it with him:

> *"Between the crosses, row on row,*
> *And in the sky, the larks*
> *Still bravely singing,*
> *Fly scarce heard amidst the guns below."*

One day I have promised myself that I will screw up my courage and walk Poppy Field with Mama. We will do it together, holding hands. And I have promised myself something else too. I will go down to Poppy Field every Christmas morning, and be there, as Papa was, and one day see this strange meeting for myself.

Papa will be with me watching.

That much I know for sure.

In Flanders Fields

By John McCrae

In Flanders fields the poppies blow

Between the crosses, row on row,

That mark our place; and in the sky

The larks, still bravely singing, fly

Scarce heard amid the guns below.

We are the Dead. Short days ago

We lived, felt dawn, saw sunset glow,

Loved and were loved, and now we lie,

In Flanders fields.

Take up our quarrel with the foe:

To you from failing hands we throw

The torch; be yours to hold it high.

If ye break faith with us who die

We shall not sleep, though poppies grow

In Flanders fields.

Afterword

By the Right Revd Nigel McCulloch KCVO

former National Chaplain of The Royal British Legion and Bishop of Manchester (Retired)

Maybe one day you will visit Flanders and see the red poppies. It is strange to think that what happened so long ago in those fields is the reason why millions of people of all ages still wear special paper poppies each November.

In the story, Martens's Papa is killed ploughing his field, and sadly this has been a real fear for farmers in Flanders over the years. Many have died accidentally setting off unexploded shells hidden in the ground. But lots of safe remains of old ammunition also get ploughed up every year; there are so many, the local farmers call that time of year the "Iron Harvest".

The area around Ypres, where the story is set, was the scene of three battles. The Third Battle of Ypres was the worst, also named Passchendaele. That was when the heaviest rains in thirty years made fields like a quicksand of mud. It was terrible.

But it was at the time of the Second Battle of Ypres that the soldier-poet, whose name was John McCrae, buried his close friend. In the story, Martens's great-grandmother, the young "poppy girl" Marie, met the poet not long after.

As John looked towards the crosses on the soldiers' graves and at the poppies nearby, and scribbled and crossed out his lines, he could not have known how world-famous his poem would become, and still is.

At the headquarters of the Royal British Legion in London, we have a copy of John's final version of the poem. It is in his best handwriting, on a neat piece of paper. And, just as in the story the untidy, stained version was very precious to Martens's family, we at the Legion cherish and take the greatest care of ours.

During that war, soldiers were allowed to write to their families and girlfriends back home – just a little letter or card, always written in pencil, to say how they were and to send their love. If they were unable to write, they would ask a friend to do it for them.

Some soldiers may have asked John McCrae to do that. He was a clever man and good with words. He also wrote short stories. And the men would have trusted him, because they knew that one day their lives might depend on his medical skills. He was a doctor, a surgeon operating in the Field Hospital.

He certainly saved the lives of some. But in those days most wounded soldiers died from serious battle injuries, despite all the doctors could do. The field hospitals lacked the medicines, hygiene, equipment and skilled knowledge that is thankfully available today. John must have been devastated he could not save his friend.

John ministered to soldiers of many nationalities. It really did seem that the whole world was at war. The British and Commonwealth forces were backed up by a Labour Corps. They were the men who carried and dragged the military equipment, heavy guns, ammunitions, supplies and everything necessary for the front lines. Many came from what were the West Indies and from countries in Africa. They suffered many casualties too.

John McCrae was a Canadian who served in his country's army alongside the British. But he also had Scottish ancestry, his grandfather having emigrated from Scotland to Canada.

When he had finished his poem about the poppies, John would almost certainly have shown it to other soldiers. Most of them had lost friends too, also buried in Flanders' fields. And his verses must have helped put into words what many of them were feeling.

Within months, in December 1915, John's poem was published in a very famous British magazine called *Punch*. Maybe that would have been the height of its fame. But it turned out to be the start of even greater things.

Sadly, John did not live to see all that. In January 1918 he died from pneumonia. So he never knew that, because of his inspiring poem, replica Flanders poppies would

soon be worn. Nor that more than a hundred years later they still are being worn each year, by millions of people of many diverse backgrounds.

To understand how and why that is so, we next need to know about a lady called Moina Michael. She lived in the United States of America, which joined the war in 1917. Lots of American soldiers fought in Flanders Field and lost their lives there.

Moina had old family links in Flanders. Prompted by that personal

connection with the war, she gave up teaching at an American university so she could help in what was called "the war effort". She became a secretary, stationed in the United States, at the YMCA Overseas War Secretaries office.

On November 9th 1918, just two days before the Armistice ending the war was signed, Moina was waiting to meet someone at a conference. Whilst waiting, she leafed through an American magazine called *Ladies' Home Journal*. In it, alongside a picture of a tragic war scene, was John McCrae's poem. Although she had come across the poem before, it now inspired her in a new way. There and then she wrote a verse expressing her response to John's words. She also dedicated herself personally, in poetry, to "keep the faith" with the fallen American soldiers, and to symbolize that promise by always wearing red poppies.

She went out and bought twenty-five silk red poppies and later handed twenty-four of them to delegates at the conference. That was the very first time, just two days before the war ended, that poppies were worn in memory of those who had lost their lives fighting in the First World War.

After that, Moina tried hard to get the United States to adopt the poppy as a memorial symbol nationally, but to no avail. After the war, back at her university teaching post in Georgia, where many disabled soldiers were enrolled, she suddenly realized that not only was it important to remember those who had been killed, it was also important not to forget the needs of the veterans, now back home from the battlefields abroad. Many of them had serious physical and mental wounds and disabilities from their experiences.

After many frustrating attempts to extend her poppy idea, Moina eventually persuaded the newly founded American Legion for veterans to adopt the poppy. It became their emblem of remembrance for every November 11th. Because of her unstinting efforts to achieve this, Moina became known in the United States as the Poppy Lady.

But Moina's story still does not explain how the poppy became so popular in the United Kingdom. That is where a French lady called Anna Guérin had an important role. She happened to be at that same American Legion conference.

Excited by the American Legion's decision – thanks to Moina – to adopt the poppy, Anna felt certain she could arrange for replica Flanders poppies to be made back in France, and sold in aid of injured veterans and the many orphaned children from the war.

Anna was also determined to push her idea widely. In 1921 she tried to persuade Australia, New Zealand, Canada and especially Britain, where she had lived for some years before the war's outbreak, to adopt the poppy as an emblem.

Now it so happened that, earlier in that same year of 1921, the British Legion had been founded as an organization to help the soldiers now back home. The sad truth was that the British public were quickly forgetting the desperate situation that many veterans and bereaved families were in. And the Legion needed to raise money fast to deal with this massive welfare task.

Anna Guérin's visit to London that year could not have been timed better. She succeeded in persuading the British Legion to have a Poppy Appeal in time for November 11th. Anna provided nine million poppies for the UK, made by French widows and orphans, in memory of those who had been killed and in support of those veterans and families who needed help. Some poppies

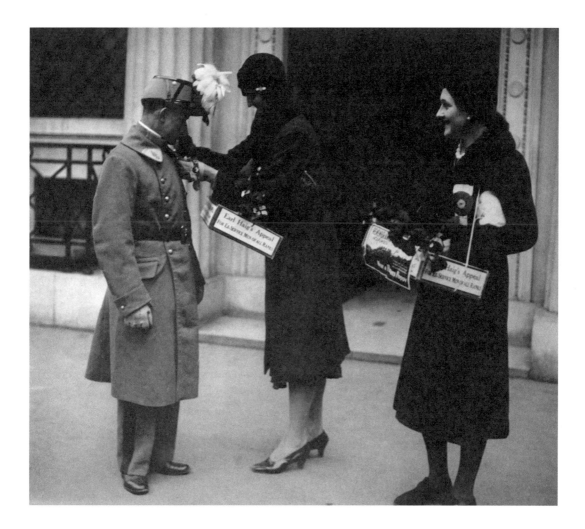

were made in silk, others in cotton. They raised the massive sum for those days of £106,000.

In the following year, the British Legion asked the Disabled Society to employ disabled veterans in England to make the poppies. One of the founders of the Disabled Society thought the previous year's success with the poppies would not be repeated. He wrote, "I do not think it can be a great success, but it is worth trying."

Well, try they did and they succeeded spectacularly. Soon 30 million

poppies a year were being sold, and the money raised enabled the British Legion to expand its much needed welfare work. By 1926 the organization had opened its poppy factory, in Richmond, London, which still employs disabled veterans to this day. In those early years, with such massive demand, it soon became impossible to make enough poppies. So another poppy factory was opened, this time in Scotland.

The Canadian soldier-poet John McCrae would surely have been pleased. After all, it was his famous wartime poem that drew so much attention to the Flanders poppies. And it was his words that inspired the American Moina Michael's idea of making the poppy into a symbol of remembrance. But it was really the French Anna Guérin who, enthused by both of them, was more responsible than anyone else for making the British custom of wearing poppies so widespread.

But all that began around a hundred years ago. The number of wounded and killed in that First World War of 1914–18 was so huge, the losses of husbands, fathers, brothers, sons and other loved ones so great, that everyone hoped it really would be the "war to end all wars".

But unfortunately that was not to be. The Second World War of 1939–45 brought again vast numbers of killed and injured, more widows and orphans. That meant a new list of names to be added to war memorials. The British Legion now faced a very big addition its welfare work.

So after 1945 the Legion decided that the replica Flanders poppies would not only be about remembering the First World War but also the Second World War, and any other conflicts that might come after. Sadly, in almost every year since 1945, British troops have lost their lives on active service.

The annual Legion Poppy Appeal is a popular occasion that draws this diverse nation together – in workplaces, communities and schools across the land. Around 45 million poppies are bought and worn each year.

Pupils have discovered through school projects, and by searching on the Internet, about family members who fought or died in past wars. Lots of British children have ancestors who lived in India, Pakistan, Bangladesh, in the Caribbean, in African countries or other faraway places, who served with the British.

Wearing a poppy helps us to remember all their sacrifices, as well as helping to raise the big sums of money that make possible the Legion's care for veterans and service families in need.

Of course the number of casualties since 1945 has thankfully been nothing like the terrible losses of the two world wars. Nowadays the field hospitals in places of conflict are incredibly better than they were long ago. The new knowledge of doctors, strict hygiene, and up-to-date equipment mean that many who previously would have died are now saved. Often they have life-changing injuries, physical or mental, that will require support for decades to come.

The poppy honours all in the Armed Forces who, in the service of the country, have lost their lives. That has nothing to do with what might be the rights or wrongs of a particular war. A century later, the nations we fought then are today our friends. The poppy is about remembering the tragic loss of life, the human cost of war. That is why people of every background are proud to wear a Legion poppy.

Each November there is a special Garden of Remembrance in the grounds of Westminster Abbey. There people can plant a Legion poppy attached to a small stick. The sticks are made in the shape of the different main faiths and none, according to personal choice.

And on Remembrance Sunday, and on November 11th, Legion poppy wreaths are laid at the foot of war memorials all over the country.

No one has to wear a poppy. Nor is there any special way in which a poppy should be worn. It was for the freedom to choose that those we remember gave their lives. So if and when you choose to wear a poppy made by the Royal British Legion, please think about its meanings.

First, we wear it to honour the memory of those who in two world wars, and other conflicts since, have lost their lives in the service of others. (At the Legion's Festival of Remembrance, shown each year on television, countless paper poppy petals float down from high up in the ceiling of the Royal Albert Hall, as another way of remembering the fallen. It is a very moving moment.)

Second, we buy poppies to raise money to help the Legion support veterans of all ages, current members of the Services, and their families who still need care and support. The Poppy Appeal is an important way of remembering those who live on.

Third, we have poppies as a sign of hope. In the story, young Marie gave the soldiers poppies from the field when she went to sell her eggs. She did it to cheer them up. She knew that the ground covered their friends who had been killed in battle, and it was a place of sadness.

But she also realized that the bright poppies that flowered so cheerfully from that soil could be seen as a sign of hope in the midst of despair.

Today, after so many wars and conflicts in the past hundred years, Marie's thoughtful gesture can be a sign to us to keep hope alive in this generation. The hope that one day wars really will stop for ever, and all the nations in the world will be reconciled and live together in peace.